Rewritten by Madge Tovey
Illustrated by Rodney Bills

Mitya lives way up north
near a big forest where it gets very cold.

One day Babushka knitted some woolly new mittens to keep Mitya's hands warm.
They were beautiful, red and white and soft.

Mitya wore his new mittens into the forest as he looked for firewood. When he stopped to tie his boot, he forgot one mitten and left it under a tree.

Soon Mouse came by shivering and shaking with the cold.
"What's this?" He sniffed the mitten.
"Something warm, just for me!"

Mouse crawled inside. He wiggled and snuggled and made himself cozy and warm.

Soon Rabbit came by shivering
and shaking with the cold.
“What’s this?” He sniffed the mitten.
“Something warm, just for me!”

“No, just for ME,” said Mouse.

"Please let me in, too," begged Rabbit. Mouse looked at Rabbit's big feet. He sighed and reluctantly moved over. Rabbit crawled inside.

Mouse and Rabbit wiggled and
snuggled and made themselves
cozy and warm.

Soon Hedgehog came by
shivering and shaking
with the cold.
"What's this?" He sniffed
the mitten. "Something
warm, just for me!"
"No, just for us," said
Mouse and Rabbit.
"Please let me in, too,"
begged Hedgehog.

Mouse and Rabbit looked at Hedgehog's prickles. They sighed and reluctantly moved over. Hedgehog crawled inside. Mouse, Rabbit, and Hedgehog wiggled and snuggled and made themselves cozy and warm.

Soon Fox came by shivering and shaking with the cold. "What's this?" He sniffed the mitten. "Something warm, just for me!"

"No, just for us," said Mouse, Rabbit, and Hedgehog. "Please let me in, too," begged Fox. Mouse, Rabbit, and Hedgehog looked at Fox's bushy tail. They sighed and reluctantly moved over. Fox crawled inside. Mouse, Rabbit, Hedgehog, and Fox wiggled and snuggled and made themselves cozy and warm.

Soon Bear came by shivering
and shaking with the cold.
"What's this?" He sniffed the
mitten. "Something warm,
just for me!"
"No, just for us," said Mouse,
Rabbit, Hedgehog, and Fox.

"Move over!" growled Bear.

Mouse, Rabbit, Hedgehog, and Fox looked at Bear's sharp claws. They sighed and reluctantly moved over. Bear crawled inside. Mouse, Rabbit, Hedgehog, Fox, and Bear wiggled and snuggled and made themselves cozy and warm.

Bear rolled over and poked Fox with one sharp claw. Fox rolled over and brushed Hedgehog with his bushy tail. Hedgehog rolled over and scratched Rabbit with his prickles. Rabbit rolled over and bumped Mouse with his big feet. Mouse rolled over and tickled Bear's nose with his long whiskers and…

Bear sneezed! "Ahh . . . ahh . . . ahh . . . Choo!"

The End